DANCE OF DEATH

A SHORT STORY

ALEXANDRIA BLAELOCK

BlueMere Books
MELBOURNE, AUSTRALIA

For permission requests, please contact
enquiries@bluemerebooks.com.

Ordering Information:
Discounts are available on quantity purchases. For details, contact orders@bluemerebooks.com.

Dance of Death/Alexandria Blaelock
paperback ISBN: 978-1-922744-45-6
digital ISBN: 978-1-922744-46-3

Book Layout © BookDesignTemplates.com
Cover Art © grandfailure/Depositphotos

DANCE OF DEATH

Death looked down the listless dry street. The sun-bleached wood of the run-down buildings was almost as white as his bones and just as glary in the sun.

What remained of the roofs were grey with lichen.

A solitary street lamp marking the coach stop leaned drunkenly on its post.

The town was as parched and dry as him.

Leaning on his scythe, he reached into his heavy black wool cowl and pulled out a plain, but serviceable wooden hourglass and held it up to his skeletal face.

Surely it was later than that?

He gave it a vigorous shake, but the build-up of sand didn't change or move any faster.

A light breeze wrapped his cowl around his legs as it lifted the red dust from one side of the street and deposited it on the other with a whisper.

He shook his leg a couple of times to free it.

God it was hot here.

Hot enough to create a Death for each and every kind of creature that died out here.

Unfortunately, without flesh or skin, he couldn't squint in the face of the relentless sun, or sweat to cool down.

He threw back his hood and scratched his skull behind the ear hole with a bony finger.

How long before the Powers That Be gave him a nice, cool Summer uniform.

Something elegant in linen would be best.

Maybe a little tailored suit, with a smooth fitted silhouette.

And a modern, streamlined watch to match.

And really, would a small, lightweight penknife he could slip in a breast pocket be too much to ask for?

But Death was halfway grateful it wasn't winter.

A few years ago, he'd lost a couple of toes when the street was boggy with red mud. Luckily, they grew back, though it was goddamned painful at the time.

Perhaps an elegant Italian leather shoe would help, though Death supposed he'd lose a whole foot in the mud that way.

He grinned at the thought of what the human archaeologists might make of digging up an Italian loafer with a skeletal foot inside.

The ghost of a Cobb & Co carriage careened down the street, its four skeletal horses skidding around the corner, narrowly missing the hotel verandah Death stood opposite.

The old Chinese man sitting on the verandah, barely started. He tamped the tobacco in his long stem clay pipe and lit it, sucking a little to draw the smoke up.

Li Quan propped his feet on the guardrails, and balanced on the back legs of the chair, idly pushing himself backwards and letting himself fall forward as he puffed.

Death checked his hourglass again and wondered if he could get away with kicking the legs out from under Quan.

A sulphur-crested cockatoo landed on the roof behind him with a thud, "G'day mate," it said as it walked along the gutter to stand more or less beside, but a little to the left of Death, "how's it hanging?"

Death turned and thrust his scythe at the bird to shoo it away, but it just lifted its yellow crest and spread its wings as it reared back, then leaned forward, folding its wings and making itself comfortable.

"As you know full well Mooyi," he said to the cockatoo, "I don't have an "it" to hang."

"Ah mate, that's harsh that is."

Death jerked the scythe again, but the bird just looked at him.

Li Quan sucked his pipe as he rocked, popping in syncopation with the creaking of the chair.

"Hello cocky," he said.

"Squawk," the cockatoo replied.

Silence, aside fromthe music Quan was making fell on the street.

He was the last man left in the town, last person if you want to be particular.

Technically he worked for Cobb & Co, running the hotel and taking care of the horses, but it had been a long time since the town was on a regular coach run.

He still cleaned the stables every morning, and lit the lamp every night as dusk fell, because even if there wasn't a coach with passengers, a rider might come by with a bag of rice, or a box of tea, or a letter.

In between, he tended his fruit and vegetable plot and distilled his own alcohols with the produce.

Or meditated and read the sutras.

But mostly just sat, looking out at the wide brown land he lived on.

Death turned away and glared into the heat haze shimmering across the far end of the street.

The shimmer intensified, and two figures emerged from within it.

One was a man with the head of an ox, and the other a man with the face of a horse.

Both were richly dressed in bright Chinese silks, padded and embroidered with gold threads into soft armour.

They carried tridents and chains, and wore swords tucked in their belts.

Worst of all, they wore long boots.

No.

Actually, worser than worst of all, they had hanging things.

Death stepped into the street between them and Quan.

"Death, be gone," said Ox-Head, "this is not your soul to collect."

Horse-Face nodded once in the affirmative.

"This is a country that believes in me," Death replied, "they don't know who you are."

"This is our soul, we will collect it," said Ox-Head, "because it is possible."

"Argh," grunted Death, "did you not hear me? This is my place, and these people don't know who you are."

Ox-Head put a hand on his sword, "Li Quan knows who we are, he is waiting for us."

Death bashed his scythe handle on the ground as another cockatoo landed on the roof of the derelict General Store.

"G'day mateys," it said.

"G'day mate," said Mooyi."

"Hello Cocky," said Quan.

Death feinted with his scythe, the bird raised its crest, flapped its wings a couple of times and jumped a little further down the street towards the animal-headed creatures.

"There's no need to be nasty," it said, "I'm just being a bit social mate."

"How is this going?" said Horse-Face.

"Hot enough for you mate?" the bird asked in reply.

Horse-Face shook his head and shrugged one shoulder.

Another cockatoo landed nearby, "all good mate?"

And another further away, "'ow ya goin' mate?"

Death's bones creaked as he tensed up.

"You right mate?" another bird asked as it landed.

Death clenched his fist.

And took a step forward as he lunged at Ox-Head who leaned to the side to dodge the punch.

Horse-Face slapped the back of Death's skull as he fell between them.

Death twisted his torso and doubled back towards Horse-Face, catching him with a one-two punch to the chest as he passed.

Horse-Face bent forward, then staggered back, trying to stay upright.

Death curled, and flipped, and leapt feet first towards Ox-Head, landing one foot to the guts as Ox-Head used the other to try to leverage Death's body into a spin away.

Death's foot came away at the ankle, and he screamed in shock and pain, landing awkwardly.

He was so angry, he swept his scythe towards Ox-Head who blocked him with his trident.

Barely hampered by his missing foot, Death squared off with Ox-Head, scythe swooping only to be met by the trident time and time again.

Horse-Face had no quarrel with Death, so he took a step back to watch the fight.

Occasionally twitching as if he was fighting too.

Quan, oblivious to the spirit plane battle in the street, put down his pipe and walked into the street.

He pulled a handful of seed from his pocket as he approached the cockatoo flock. "Hello cocky," he said again.

A couple of birds flew closer, watching him carefully.

Mooyi landed on his shoulder and rubbed his cheek against Quan's.

"G'day mate," he said, and Quan laughed as he reached out to scratch the back of the bird's neck.

"G'day you too."

Quan spread the seed on the General Store balustrade for the birds to eat, then took an apple and a penknife from his other pocket and carved a piece off for Mooyi.

As Mooyi started nibbling it, he carved a piece for himself to eat as well.

As the spirit fight intensified, he leaned up against the verandah post and watched the birds eat.

"Pretty birdie," he said, and one or another cockatoo squawked back.

Ox-Head twisted away, Death kicked him in the back of the knee with the stump of his leg.

As Ox-Head fell, Death's scythe sliced through the air and severed Quan's soul from his body.

Mooyi squawked and flew to the roof as Quan's body fell to the ground startling the cockatoos.

The rest of the flock launched upwards, screeching, in all directions.

The soul collectors were fully immersed by the fight and didn't notice the commotion.

Quan looked down at his body slumped on the ground, and then became aware of the fight going on in front of him.

His eyes widened, and his spirit hands flew to his mouth.

Of course he recognised Ox-Head and Horse-Face as the guardians of Diyu, there to take him before the courts of Hell.

But he had no idea who the robed skeleton was or why it was trying to prevent his justice.

He was more afraid than he had ever been while alive.

What would happen to him if he wasn't judged and punished according to the requirements of the sutras?

As Quan shrank back, Horse-Face leapt to Ox-Head's defence.

Quan felt as though all his future lives were blowing away from him like the red dirt in the wind.

While he was prepared to take the punishment he deserved, all he wanted was to stay in this place where he'd been so happy.

He'd defied his parents and village, and stayed many long years after they'd demanded he return.

A hairy black hand touched his shoulder for a moment, and he was infused with calm.

Wordlessly, the creature invited him to join the other souls from this place, and he readily agreed.

One by one, the cockatoos landed on and around Quan's body, and quietly watched the fight.

As Death twisted out from under Horse-Face's sword, he noticed the body.

He allowed the Chinese soul collectors to dismember his skeleton, barely flinching before he pulled himself together.

"Did something happen to Quan?" Death asked.

"Yeah, nah," said Mooyi, "the Yowie took 'im."

"The Yowie?"

"Yeah mate, the Yowie."

"What is this Yowie to do with Li Quan?" asked Ox-Head.

"Ah well," said Mooyi shrugging, "youse made him mad."

"Mad?" asked Horse-Face.

"Yeah mate, mad."

"Mooyi," said Death through gritted teeth, "if you don't tell me what happened to Quan this instant, so help me, I'll take you to Hell and see you stay there."

"Nah mate, you can't do that, I don't belong to you."

"Mooyi."

"All right mate, no need to get your knickers in a knot."

The cockatoos fell about laughing, and Death poked his scythe at them.

"Nah mate, it's not very respectful, is it?"

"What is your respect for this?" asked Ox-Head.

"Well, all this fighting about jurisdictions in front of the soul."

"Jurisdiction?"

"Yeah mate, jurisdiction."

"Jur-is-dic-tion," said Horse-Face as if he didn't know what the word meant.

"Yeah mate, you can't be fighting about who a soul belongs to when it's standing right there watchin' ya."

"Watching?"

"Yeah mate, he was watchin' youse fight over him."

"I do not understand," said Ox-Head.

"It's really very simple," said Death, "while we were fighting, this Yowie stole Quan's soul out from under us."

"That's right mate."

Death rubbed his skull above his eye sockets with his right thumb and middle finger, "by what reason does this Yowie have the first claim?"

"Ah mate! How long 'ave ya been coming here and ya still have no idea have ya?"

Death scuffed a toe in the dirt.

"Yowie took the first soul from this place to live in the Land of the Sky People."

Ox-Head gently scratched the back of his head with one of the points of his trident, "Yowie brought Li Quan to the air?"

"Yeah mate."

"Can we let him come back?"

"Nah mate, he's gone now. Just like when you take 'em to Diyu."

"While I concede that perhaps Yowie has jurisdiction, I'm not clear on why he took Quan," said Death

"Because Quan wanted 'im to, mate."

"Wanted him to?"

"Yeah mate, said 'e belonged here mate."

"Once belonged to here?" asked Horse-Face.

"Yeah mate, said this was 'is place."

Ox-Head looked at Horse-Face, "King Yama is not happy."

Horse-Face nodded, "There will paperwork there because it doesn't exist here?"

"I should think so, mate."

"One thing's for sure," said Death, "we can't be going around letting souls decide what happens to them, can we?"

The Chinese soul collectors shook their heads.

"Higher than my pay grade," said Ox-Head, "but I will pass it back."

"Do," said Death, "I'll recommend treaty negotiations commence immediately," and winked out.

Ox-Head turned to Horse-Face, "maybe it will be fine, King Yama likes paperwork."

"Also hope so," Horse-Face replied.

The air shimmered around them, and they disappeared into the haze.

"Well, that went well, eh mate?" asked Mooyi.

"Sure did, mate. Fancy a snack?"

"Yeah, I reckon. Gum tree mate?"

"Sounds good mate, I'll race ya."

A flurry of wings stirred the air, and the flock took to the sky, calling out to each other as they flew.

Back on the ground, the dust settled and lay still.

THE END

ABOUT THE AUTHOR

Alexandria Blaelock writes stories, some of them for *Ellery Queen's Mystery Magazine* and *Pulphouse Fiction Magazine*.

She's also written five self-help books applying business techniques to personal matters like getting dressed, cleaning house, and feeding your friends.

Discover more at www.alexandriablaelock.com.

BOOKS BY
ALEXANDRIA BLAELOCK

SHORT STORY COLLECTIONS

The Histories of Hayward Hall
Lovelorn, Lovestruck and Love at First Sight
Common or Garden Variety Heroes
Case Files of the Wilkinson Detective Agency
Unavoidable Fates
Christmas Travesties
Five Faces of Felicia Clarke

OTHER FICTION

That Love Nonsense
Taipan vs Brown

MS BLAELOCK'S BOOKS

Stress Free Dinner Parties
Signature Wardrobe Planning
Holistic Personal Finance
Minimally Viable Housekeeping
Planning a Life Worth Living

SELECTED SHORT STORIES

Alma's Grace
Balancing the Book
Carmelita Basingstoke
Fate in Your Hands
Kiss of Death
Lady of the Looking Glass
Life in the Security Directorate
Long Weekend in the Snow
Love in the Past Tense
Love in the Security Directorate
Morning Star, Evening Star, Superstar
Needy Bitch
Payton's Run
Phoenix Child
Secret Singer
Shining Star
Ship in a Bottle
Simone Says Hands in the Air
Special Relativity in Space
The Bygone Boyfriend
The Day the Schedule Broke
The Ghost Detectors
The Guardian's Vigil
The Mince Pie Mystery
The Mystery of the Master Suite
The Pseudonym's Bride
The Shadow Thieves
The Space-Time Paradox
Toy Soldiers